The Littles
Give a Party

BY **JOHN PETERSON**
PICTURES BY **ROBERTA CARTER CLARK**

SCHOLASTIC INC.
New York Toronto London Auckland Sydney Tokyo

To my grandmothers

ISBN 0-590-41988-9

Text copyright © 1972 by John Peterson. Illustrations copyright © 1972 by Scholastic Inc. All rights reserved. Published by Scholastic Inc.

12 11 10 9 8 7 6 5 4 3 2   0 1 2 3/9

"MISSISSIPPI is a long word," said Tom Little. "How do you spell it?"

"Well now, let's see," said Uncle Pete. "I used to be pretty good at spelling when I was a boy." He scratched his moustache and looked up at the living room ceiling. "M-i-s-s-i-s-s-i-p-p-i."

"Wrong!" said ten-year-old Tom. He was grinning.

"Wrong?" said Uncle Pete. "Now how could that be wrong? I've never had any trouble spelling Mississippi that I can remember."

Tom's eight-year-old sister, Lucy, was trying to keep from laughing. She was standing behind Granny Little's rocking chair so that Uncle Pete wouldn't see her. The old woman was rocking slowly back and forth.

"I didn't ask you how to spell Mississippi," said Tom. "I asked you how to spell *it!*"

Uncle Pete's eyebrows went up.

"Remember?" said Tom. "I said, 'Mississippi is a *long word!* How do you spell *it?*'"

"Ho! Ho!" said Uncle Pete. He slapped his knee. "That's a good one, Tom!"

Lucy came out from behind Granny Little's chair. "Wasn't that funny, Granny — the way Tom fooled Uncle Pete?"

Granny Little turned to Lucy. "Were you talking to me, Lucy?"

"Don't you think Tom's joke was funny?" said Lucy.

"I'm sorry, Lucy," said the old woman. "I wasn't listening."

Tom was sitting next to Uncle Pete on the sofa. "There — did you hear her?" he whispered. "Granny did it again. She's not paying any attention to what people say."

Uncle Pete shook his head. "No — she's hard of hearing, that's all."

"No sir!" Tom said. "Granny is not even *trying* to listen. That's the trouble!"

The Littles were tiny people. The tallest Little was Tom's and Lucy's father, Mr. William T. Little. And he was only six inches tall. The tiny Littles lived in a small ten-room apartment inside the walls of a house owned by Mr. George Bigg. Mr. Bigg was a regular-sized person. He and his wife and their son, Henry, never knew the Littles were living in the same house with them. The Littles were careful not to show themselves when the Biggs were around.

Even though they were small, the Littles looked mostly like ordinary people. The one difference was — the Littles had tails! The tails weren't useful. They just looked good, the Littles thought.

Later in the day, the Little children were playing follow-the-leader in the Biggs' attic.

Tom hopped up on a stack of old newspapers. Lucy followed. "What's wrong with Granny Little, Tom?" she said.

Tom climbed from the newspapers to the top of a suitcase. "I don't know," he said, "but she doesn't act at all like she usually does. Golly! She's not paying any attention to anybody!"

Lucy stood on the suitcase behind Tom. She teetered, arms out to help her balance.

Tom walked on the suitcase, trying to stay on the zipper. Then he turned and

leaped into space, bouncing on a mattress below. Lucy was right behind him.

"Granny's sad about something — that's what I think," Lucy said. She sat beside Tom on the mattress.

"I wonder what," Tom said.

"Maybe we can make her happy again if we try," said Lucy.

"Hey!" Tom hopped to his feet on the spongy mattress. "It's almost dinnertime. Let's see what the Biggs are eating." The tiny boy somersaulted twelve times to the end of the mattress. He jumped to the floor of the attic.

"That's not fair — somersaulting makes me dizzy!" said Lucy. "You know that. I can't do it. I give up!" She climbed down from the mattress and ran to catch up with Tom.

The children took the Littles' tin-can elevator down to the Biggs' kitchen. The elevator went between the walls of the house. It was made from an old soup can and some pieces of string the Littles had gotten from the Biggs.

The Littles took everything they needed from the Biggs: scraps of cloth, old socks, handkerchiefs and ribbons to make into clothes, empty match boxes and cigar boxes for furniture, birthday candles and Christmas bulbs for lights.

Usually the things they took were so small and unimportant, the Biggs never missed them. Now and then something caused a stir. Just yesterday, Henry Bigg yelled, "Someone stole my blue jay feather!"

Mrs. Bigg said, "No one stole anything, Henry. I'll help you find the feather."

They looked all over but they never found Henry's blue jay feather. It was still in the Biggs' house though. Lucy thought Henry was finished with it, so she had taken it. It was too late to return the feather when Lucy found out Henry still wanted it. She had already pulled it apart, throwing away the hard spine. Lucy was making a feather pillow to give to Granny Little for her birthday.

And of course the Littles got all their food from the Biggs. Whatever the Biggs had for dinner, the Littles had for dinner too, *if* they could sneak it out of the kitchen.

The Biggs didn't know about it, but the electric socket over the kitchen counter was a secret door. The Littles could slip through the secret socket door and carry off any leftovers they wanted for their meals.

Now Tom and Lucy were standing behind the socket. They could see through the slots into the kitchen.

"Do you see what I see, Lucy?" asked Tom.

"It's Granny Little's favorite dessert!" said Lucy.

"Yep!" Tom said. "Rice pudding with

raisins. Granny says no one makes it as good as Mrs. Biggs does. And she hasn't made it for months."

"Won't Granny be happy?" said Lucy. "I can hardly wait to see her face."

"Well," Tom said, "I'm going to get some for her."

"Oh — you should wait for Daddy or Mommy," said Lucy. "You know they don't want us to go after food alone."

"If we wait until the Biggs are finished eating," Tom said, "there may not be any. You know how Mr. Bigg likes it. And that Henry! He's a hog about rice pudding!"

"You should wait!" said Lucy.

Tom looked around for Mrs. Bigg. "There — she's out of the room. I'll just run out and scoop up three pieces of rice and a raisin before she gets back," he said. He picked up an empty bottle cap to use as a plate. Mrs. Little always kept a supply of bottle caps near the secret door.

"No, Tom!" Lucy said, but Tom

wouldn't listen. He pushed open the electric socket door and slipped through to the kitchen counter. He ran toward the rice pudding. Then, suddenly, he stopped.

The lid was off the peanut butter jar.

Now Tom Little loved peanut butter more than any other food in the world. And because the lid was usually on the jar, and the jar in the cupboard, he *never* got enough of it.

Henry Bigg probably had a snack and forgot to put the lid back on. That was usual. The *unusual* thing was that Mrs. Bigg hadn't yet spotted it.

Tom looked at the rice pudding. He looked at the open peanut butter jar. Then he looked around for Mrs. Bigg. He just might have time to get both, he thought. It was a chance to catch up on his peanut butter eating.

Tom turned and dashed for the open jar.

It was too high!

Tom pushed an apple off a plate of fruit. He rolled it to the peanut butter jar. Then he pulled himself up onto the apple, using it for a stool.

When Tom leaned over the edge and smelled the fresh roasted peanut smell, he said: "Oh!" and "Wow!" He reached way down into the jar to scoop out some peanut butter. But he couldn't quite reach it.

Tom stood high on his toes and tried again. Suddenly the apple rolled out from under his feet. Tom tried to balance himself on the lip of the jar. But he couldn't: he was too far over the lip. Down he slid, right into the sticky peanut butter.

TOM Little was on his knees in the
peanut butter. He reached up but he
couldn't reach the lip of the jar. He tried
to stand. The peanut butter was like
quicksand: it held him down. Every time
Tom moved he sank deeper into the
peanut butter.

Tom was scared. He had to get out of
the jar before Mrs. Bigg saw him. Or what
if she didn't see him and put the lid on
the jar! He would suffocate to death!

Just then Henry Bigg came into the kitchen. He walked to the counter where Tom was trapped. "Hey, Mom!" called Henry. "Can I have another little peanut butter sandwich?"

"No, Henry, you may not," said Mrs. Bigg from the other room. "You'll ruin your appetite. We're going to have dinner soon."

Mrs. Bigg came to the kitchen door. "And please put the lid back on the peanut butter," she said. Then she picked up some dishes and carried them from the room.

Tom was terrified. He tried to call out to Henry Bigg not to put the lid on the jar. But he was so frightened he couldn't make a sound.

Henry picked up a spoon. He kept his eyes on the door. "OK, Mom," he said. Then slowly, Henry stuck the spoon into the peanut butter jar. He kept looking at the door.

The spoon came down toward Tom in the jar. Tom saw a way to escape. He grabbed the spoon just as Henry scooped up some peanut butter on it.

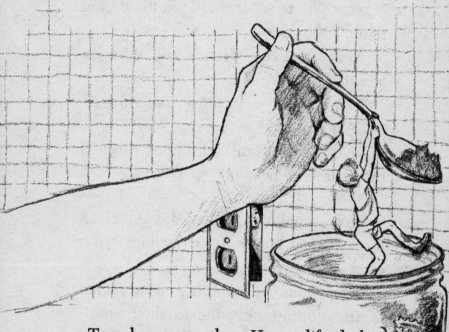

Tom hung on when Henry lifted the spoonful of peanut butter. As soon as the spoon came out of the jar, Tom let go and dropped to the counter. Then he ran around behind the jar and hid.

Henry had not even seen Tom. He was busy watching for his mother. He shoved the spoonful of peanut butter into his mouth.

"Come here, Henry!" It was Mrs. Bigg. "I want you to set the table in the dining room."

"Yesh, Muvver," Henry said with his mouth full.

"Henry! Are you eating something?"

Gulp! "Nope!"

By this time Tom had slipped through the secret socket door to safety.

"Tom," said Mrs. Little, "did you clean the peanut butter from behind your ears?"

It was later. All the Littles were seated at the diningroom table in their apartment between the walls. They were eating the leftovers from the Biggs' dinner.

"Aw, cut it out, will you, Mom?" said Tom.

"Boys will be boys, I always say," said Uncle Pete. "Tom's a good lad. He just can't resist peanut butter."

Baby Betsy, who was seven months old, sat in her high chair and smiled at everyone. Mrs. Little was feeding her bread crumbs soaked in a drop of milk. "Anyway, Tom — I hope you got enough peanut butter to last you for a while," she said.

"Mother!" said Tom.

Mr. Little spoke: "Tom didn't get *any* peanut butter," he said. "He was much too worried during the whole adventure to think about eating."

"Oh dear!" said Mrs. Little. "That's too bad, Tom."

Uncle Pete laughed. "Boys will be boys," he said again.

"What does that mean, Uncle Pete?" said Lucy.

"Well, Lucy, it simply means ... ah ..." Uncle Pete looked around the table for someone to help him answer the question. "Well *everyone* knows what that means, Lucy."

"I don't."

Uncle Pete cleared his throat. He stood up, picked up his cane, and limped over to the fireplace. (Uncle Pete had been wounded in the Mouse Invasion of '35.) He banged his cane on the floor as he walked. Then he turned to Granny Little. "*You* tell Lucy what I mean, Granny! By gum, you're the one who's always saying, 'Boys will be boys.' "

Granny Little didn't say anything. She stared straight ahead.

"Granny!" Uncle Pete spoke louder.

Granny Little looked up. "Were you saying something to me, Peter?" she said. "I wasn't listening."

The Littles looked at Granny Little. There was a long silence.

Lucy spoke quietly. "Does it mean

something like, 'Boys are rotten, made of cotton'?"

"Yes, yes, that's it!" Uncle Pete said. He began limping back and forth. "It means boys will get in trouble if they are real boys."

"That's a silly saying," said Mrs. Little. "Tom is a good boy." She patted her son on the cheek. "He hardly ever gets into trouble."

Mr. Little got up and left the room. He returned with a bottle cap full of Mrs. Bigg's rice pudding. "Surprise, Granny!" He placed the dessert in front of Granny Little.

The old woman looked down at the rice pudding. "I'm not very hungry, Will, if you don't mind," she said. Then she stood up. "And I'm quite tired. If you will excuse me, I'll go lie down for a while."

"But Granny!" said Tom. "It's your *favorite* dessert!"

"Is it?" said Granny Little. She looked at the rice pudding. "So it is. Oh well — these days one dessert is just as good as another, I suppose." She walked slowly from the room.

"Something's bothering her," said Mrs. Little, "and I'm going to find out what it is." She got up from the table and followed Granny Little to her bedroom.

"HER birthday?" said Uncle Pete. He laughed. "And I thought there was something wrong with her."

"Keep your voice down, please, Uncle Pete," said Mrs. Little. "Granny may hear you."

The Littles were gathered in the living room after dinner. Lucy was rocking Baby Betsy in her matchbox cradle. Mr. Little turned on a yellow Christmas tree bulb. Uncle Pete stood by the fireplace twirling his cane.

"Granny Little is depressed," Mrs. Little went on, "because she's going to be eighty years old on the Fourth of July."

"What's so bad about that?" said Uncle Pete.

"Granny says that when she was a little girl she made up her mind to live to be eighty," Mrs. Little said. "Now she will be eighty this coming Monday, and she says it's too old."

"Too old for what, for heaven's sake?" said Uncle Pete. "Being eighty doesn't stop her. She does almost everything we do. She ought to be happy! I hope *I* live to be eighty!"

"I hope you live to be eighty too, Uncle Pete!" said Lucy.

Uncle Pete began walking back and forth. "It's dangerous being a tiny person," he said. "It's a hard life! Why, it's amazing that Granny Little has lived to be eighty years old." He turned to Tom. "Did you know your great grandmother lived through the Mouse Invasion of '35?"

"Sit down, will you please, Uncle Pete?" said Mrs. Little. "You're making me nervous."

"Umph!" said Uncle Pete. He sat down hard on his favorite chair near the fireplace.

"We'll have to find a way to cheer Granny up," said Mr. Little.

"I don't think Granny Little is too old," Tom said. "Golly, she does as much work as anyone. And she's lots of fun!"

"I'm sorry Granny Little is so old," said Lucy. Suddenly she ran to her mother. "Will she die soon?"

Uncle Pete got out of his chair and began walking again.

Mrs. Little put her arm around Lucy. "No, Lucy," she said. "Your great grandmother is strong and in good health. We just have to keep her that way."

"I'll go and talk to her," said Uncle Pete. "I'll just say, 'Now see here, Granny — stop this nonsense! You're as fit as a fiddle!' I'll tell her she's in perfect health and she's going to live for years and years." He started toward the door, then stopped and turned around. "That will work, won't it?"

"No, Uncle Pete, I don't think that will help," said Mrs. Little. "Instead of telling her, we have to show her, somehow, that her eightieth birthday is something to be glad about and not something to hate."

"I like birthdays," Lucy said. "I wish Granny Little liked her birthday."

"She has a keen birthday," said Tom. "Even Mr. Bigg stays home from work on the Fourth of July — Granny's birthday. It's Independence Day!"

"*Everybody* stays home on the Fourth of July," said Lucy.

"No," said Uncle Pete. "Everybody goes swimming on the Fourth of July. They go swimming and they have a picnic."

Mrs. Little sighed. "Wouldn't it be wonderful if *we* could go swimming and have a picnic on Granny's birthday," she said.

Mr. Little leaned back in his chair and smiled. "Perhaps that could be arranged, my dear Mrs. Little," he said.

"Daddy!" said Lucy. She leaped to her feet. "Could we?"

"I think," said Mr. Little, "that it is very important that we invite all of Granny's friends and relatives to a big surprise party for her. Then she will know, once and for all, that she is a very, very special person."

"And that we love her!" Lucy said.

"Amen," said Uncle Pete.

"WHOOPEE!" shouted Tom.

"Hush, Tom!" said Mr. Little. "Do you want the Biggs to know we're here?"

IT was twelve o'clock noon the next day. Uncle Pete, Mr. Little, Lucy, and Tom were on the roof of the Biggs' house. They were going to send out the invitations to Granny Little's surprise birthday party.

"Lucky for us the sun is shining," said Tom. He looked up and squinted. "We'll be able to send the messages."

"Tom, I hope you remember the code," Mr. Little said. "We want our guests to come on the right day."

"Don't worry, Dad," said Tom. "I know

the code. For the fourth you use four dots and one dash — that's the number four."

"Now step out of the way a moment, folks," Uncle Pete said. "Let me get this mirror aimed toward the east."

Uncle Pete had a small pocket mirror that Mrs. Bigg no longer used. He leaned the mirror against the top of the roof and tilted it toward the sun. The sun reflected off the mirror. It made a small spot of light on the Biggs' yard below.

When Uncle Pete moved the mirror, the spot of light moved quickly across the lawn. It streaked through the nearby woods.

Now the Littles could see the light spot on the wall of the house where their friends, the Shorts lived.

It was exactly twelve noon. The Littles knew that there were tiny people with mirrors on rooftops all over the Big Valley. Twelve o'clock was Mirror Message Time. With the sun right overhead, a message could be sent in almost any direction.

A bright flash of light came from near the chimney of the house across the woods.

"Dash-dot-dash!" said Tom. "That's a 'K,' and it means we should go ahead with our message."

"Tom — I admire you!" Uncle Pete said. "How do you remember all those dots and dashes?"

"It's easy, Uncle Pete," Tom said. "I have them all memorized from Henry Bigg's Boy Scout manual."

"Send the message, Tom," Mr. Little said. "The Shorts are waiting."

Tom was wearing a cape. When he stood by the side of the mirror and held his arm out, the cape covered the mirror. That kept the light from going to the Shorts. Every time Tom lowered his arm he made the light flash toward them.

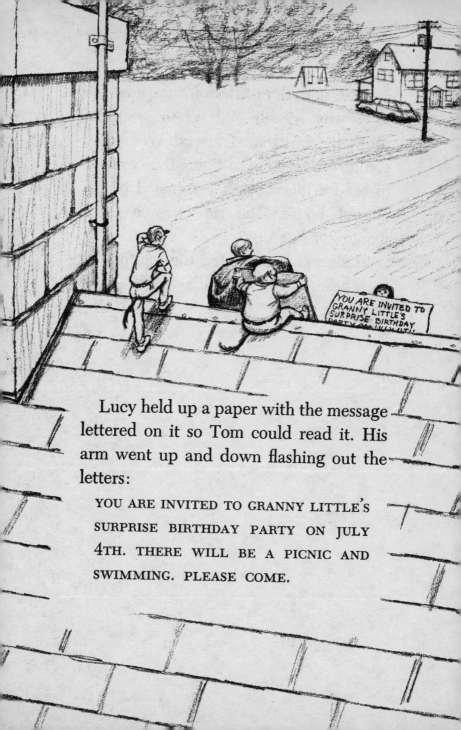

Lucy held up a paper with the message lettered on it so Tom could read it. His arm went up and down flashing out the letters:

YOU ARE INVITED TO GRANNY LITTLE'S SURPRISE BIRTHDAY PARTY ON JULY 4TH. THERE WILL BE A PICNIC AND SWIMMING. PLEASE COME.

After that, the Littles sent the message to nearby friends and relatives in the north, the south, and the west. When they couldn't see the house where they wanted to send a message, they signaled to the nearest house. The tiny people there would send it on.

Flashes of light dotted the rooftops of the houses of the Big Valley for the next hour.

THE next morning Tom and Lucy were watching the Biggs eat breakfast. They looked through the slots in the secret socket door.

"It's hot in here with that toaster plugged in," whispered Lucy.

"We're lucky," Tom said. "Sometimes they have the dishwasher plugged in too."

"Look, Tom!" whispered Lucy. "Henry!"

"Sh!" said Tom. "I'm watching."

Henry Bigg picked up a cereal box and poured some cereal into a bowl.

"The box is almost empty," said Tom.

Henry put the box down on the edge of the table.

"Now you can see the finger puppets on the back of the box," said Lucy.

"Hey — yeah!" said Tom. "They *are* keen!" Then he turned away and walked down the wall passageway.

Lucy ran after her brother. "Well, Tom?" she said. "Can we get the puppets do you think?"

Tom stopped. "The box still has some cereal in it," Tom said. "But they will probably finish eating what's left in time for us to get the box before Granny Little's birthday."

"Good!"

"Lucy, are you sure they will work?" said Tom.

"They're just plain finger puppets," said Lucy. "We'll use them for costumes."

"But they're flat," said Tom.

"Didn't you see the tabs on the side?"

said Lucy. "They fit together and make a
circle like a ring to go on the finger of the
big kids. They'll make perfect costumes
for us. We'll just put the tabs around our
waists like belts."

"Isn't Granny Little too old for a Little
Red Riding Hood play?"

"No one is too old for plays, Tom," said Lucy, "and everyone loves Little Red Riding Hood. We can get Uncle Pete to take the part of the wolf. Wouldn't he be great as a wolf?"

"OK," said Tom. "We'll do it!"

"Granny will love it, Tom."

"Let's hope the Biggs eat the cereal between now and the day before Granny's party. We'll need time to rehearse."

"I wish we could think of a way to get the box now," said Lucy. "Can't we spill the cereal on the floor or something — spoil it?"

"Lucy!" said Tom. "You know we aren't allowed to do a thing like that. Come on — let's go home and write the play."

BAD news flashed to the Littles during Mirror Message Time that day. Granny Little's old friend, Zelda Short, wasn't coming to the birthday party. And neither were Cousin Tracy and Cousin Emma, Granny's oldest living relatives. Even her sister, Littebit, sent a message that she wouldn't be there.

"For heaven's sake why, Uncle Pete?" said Mr. Little.

Uncle Pete had been on the roof with Tom getting the messages.

"We're not going to have a party," Lucy said. She pouted.

Uncle Pete put his finger to his lips. "Shhhh!" He limped to the door of Granny Little's bedroom. "Good! She's still taking her nap," he said.

"But *why*, Uncle Pete?" said Mrs. Little. "Did they say why they wouldn't come?"

"Too old!" said Uncle Pete. He shook his head. "Too old to make the trip. They say it will be too hard and too long. Fooey! I say there's no goat like an old goat! You're as young as you feel! Being too old would never stop me!"

"Darn it!" Tom said. "I hope I never get old! Old people are afraid."

"That's not true, Tom," said Mrs. Little. "They just don't have the energy for all the things they want to do, that's all." She turned to her husband. "It is true that the trip would be harder for the older people. And most tiny families aren't as lucky as we are. We have the Biggs' cat, Hildy, to travel comfortably on."

Mr. Little and Uncle Pete started to talk at the same time.

"Are you thinking what I'm thinking, Will?" said Uncle Pete.

"You mean — Cousin Dinky?"

"Yes!" said Uncle Pete. He was excited. "He could *fly* the old folks in his glider."

"What could be easier *and* more comfortable?" said Mr. Little.

"Oh dear," said Mrs. Little. "Cousin Dinky and Della are on their honeymoon. It wouldn't be fair to call them back."

"Bah!" said Uncle Pete. "They've been shilly-shallying long enough. Dinky's the mailman for the Big Valley, isn't he? Well, I've got letters I want sent. If he isn't going to get back to work, I may have to get my hands on a glider and fly the mail myself!"

"This is an emergency, Mother!" said Tom. "We need Cousin Dinky."

Lucy began skipping around the room.

"Oh good!" she said. "Cousin Dinky can fly the old people to Granny's party."

"Before everyone gets too excited," said Mrs. Little, "we ought to find out if they are willing to fly to the party in Cousin Dinky's glider. I don't think *I* would!"

"Oh heck, that's easy," said Tom. "All the old people like Cousin Dinky. They'll fly all right."

Uncle Pete said: "I too was admired by the old folks when I was Dinky's age. Isn't it remarkable how much alike we are? I suppose it's because we are both the adventurous type."

"Granny Little thinks he's super," Lucy said.

Just then the old woman came into the room from her bedroom. "Who do I think is super, Lucy? she said.

"Were you listening, Granny?" Uncle Pete said.

"Listening to what, Peter Little?" said Granny Little. "What's going on here?"

Mrs. Little took Granny Little's arm. She walked with her to the rocking chair. "We were talking about how much you enjoyed a visit from Cousin Dinky," said Mrs. Little.

"Is he coming?" said Granny Little. "I thought he and Della were still on their honeymoon."

Uncle Pete started for the door. "I'm going up on the roof and send out a message for Dinky now," he said. He looked at the pocket watch over the mantelpiece. "There's still time, Tom. Come with me."

"You may get Cousin Dinky to come," said Mrs. Little, "but I don't know whether *certain* people are brave enough to fly in his glider. I don't think I am."

Granny Little turned her head to hear. "Fly?" she said. "Did you say 'fly'? I'm going to ask Dinky why he doesn't take me up in his glider one time before I die."

Lucy Little put her head in her great grandmother's lap. "You're *never* going to die, Granny," she said. "I love you too much."

Granny Little stroked Lucy's hair. "I am going to be eighty years old on the Fourth of July. That's old enough for anyone."

LATE that afternoon Tom and Uncle
Pete were on the Biggs' porch roof. The
porch roof was not so steep as the roof of
the main house. Tom thought it would be
a good place to hold the picnic.

"And there's plenty of shade," Tom
said. He pointed to a tree whose branches
hung low over the roof.

"It's a pretty spot, Tom," said Uncle
Pete. "The ladies will particularly enjoy
the lovely white flowers on this catalpa
tree."

"And look here, Uncle Pete," said Tom. He ran to the edge of the roof. "We can dam up this rain gutter and make a place to swim." He looked up at the sky. "*If* it rains."

Uncle Pete looked at the rain gutter. "Tom — that will make a good swimming pool," he said. Then he laughed. "It's quite a bit longer than it is wide. I suppose we'll have to have two-man races."

"Do you think it will rain, Uncle Pete?" said Tom.

"If it doesn't," said Uncle Pete, "I think I know a good way to get water into it." He turned to go. "Let's get back to the others. We're going to need help to get this new swimming pool ready for us to swim in it."

"Wait a second, Uncle Pete, will you?" said Tom. He ran to a branch of the catalpa tree that hung almost to the roof. "I want to get one of these flowers for Granny Little."

Tom jumped up and grabbed a blossom from the tree. A huge bumblebee tumbled from the blossom. It was larger than Tom's head.

"Watch out, Tom!" yelled Uncle Pete. Tom dropped the blossom and ran. The bumblebee buzzed after him. Uncle Pete ran to help. He swung at the creature with his cane. "Get away!" he cried. "If that thing bites you, you're dead!"

The bumblebee streaked away. It hung over the roof a few feet away buzzing loudly.

"Run, Tom! Run!" Uncle Pete yelled. "I'll fight it off!"

The bee came toward them faster than they could see. It hit Uncle Pete's hat, knocking it off his head.

Uncle Pete swung his cane wildly even after the bee had moved away. He saw that Tom was still by his side. "Tom — get away from here!" he cried.

"I'm sticking with you, Uncle Pete," Tom said.

"It will attack again," said Uncle Pete. "We've got to find a place to hide."

The buzzing grew louder.

"Here it comes!" yelled Tom. He dropped to his knees.

Just then Tom and Uncle Pete heard a loud yell. A dark shadow flew over them. There was a rush of wind.

It was Cousin Dinky's glider skimming low over their heads. The one-winged blue and silver glider swung up and over in a loop. It zoomed down toward the

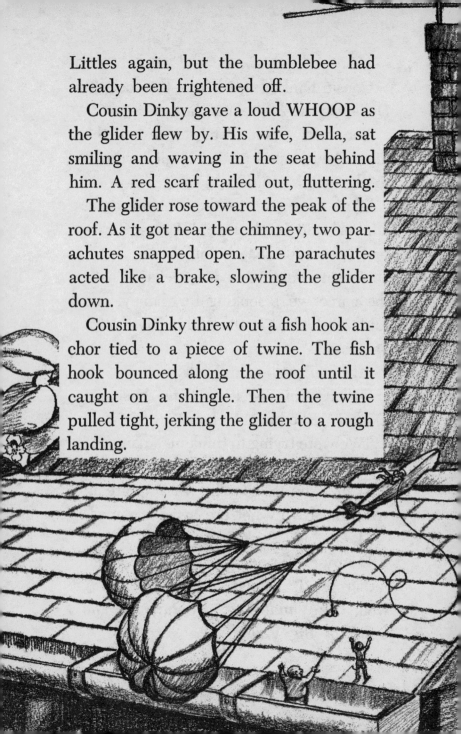

Littles again, but the bumblebee had already been frightened off.

Cousin Dinky gave a loud WHOOP as the glider flew by. His wife, Della, sat smiling and waving in the seat behind him. A red scarf trailed out, fluttering.

The glider rose toward the peak of the roof. As it got near the chimney, two parachutes snapped open. The parachutes acted like a brake, slowing the glider down.

Cousin Dinky threw out a fish hook anchor tied to a piece of twine. The fish hook bounced along the roof until it caught on a shingle. Then the twine pulled tight, jerking the glider to a rough landing.

Cousin Dinky leaped from the cockpit. Della was right behind him.

Tom and Uncle Pete ran across the roof. They helped to tie the glider down so the wind couldn't blow it away.

"You were just in the nick of time, Dinky!" said Uncle Pete. "We were in a bad spot with that bumblebee."

Cousin Dinky turned to Della. "That's the name we're looking for, honey!" he said. He looked at the glider. *The Nick of Time.*"

"It's perfect!" said Della.

"What's this 'Nick of Time' business, Dinky?" asked Uncle Pete.

"We were trying to think up a name for the new glider," said Cousin Dinky. "*The Nick of Time* seems to be what we are always in, so why not use it for a name?"

"I love it!" said Della.

"I myself," said Uncle Pete, "would rather see it named... ah, let's see... well, *The Wandering Adventurer*, or *The Spirit of Big Valley*."

Della laughed. "Oh, Uncle Pete!" she said. "You are so romantic! So old-fashioned!"

"Umph!" Uncle Pete said. "What's wrong with that?"

"Not a thing, Uncle Pete." Cousin Dinky gave Uncle Pete's arm a squeeze. "Old-fashioned is fine. Especially when it's some good old-fashioned cooking! You don't happen to know what Mrs. Bigg has planned for dinner, do you?"

"Potted chicken and rice," said Tom.

"Oh — wow!" said Cousin Dinky. "What are we waiting for?" He walked toward the secret trap door shingle in the roof. "We can talk about Granny Little's surprise birthday party later. Let's get some of those delicious leftovers."

Uncle Pete limped along behind. "*The Nick of Time* indeed!" he said. "Silly name!"

"WOULD you care for some more chicken and rice, Cousin Dinky?" asked Mrs. Little.

"Just a bit, Auntie," Cousin Dinky held out his plate.

Baby Betsy was sitting in her high chair next to Uncle Pete. He was feeding her banana and milk.

"Goo, goo!" Baby Betsy said.

"Ah, she wants more," said Uncle Pete. He cut a piece off the banana slice.

"How can you tell, Uncle Pete?" said Lucy.

" 'Goo goo' means 'food,' Lucy," said Uncle Pete.

Tom laughed. "I thought goo was sticky stuff."

"Right, Tom!" said Uncle Pete. "Goo is sticky stuff, and goo goo is sticky food."

All the Littles laughed except Granny ·Little. She sat staring at her plate, not eating. Della sat next to her. "Can I get you something else to eat, Granny?" she asked.

"What?" said Granny Little. She looked at Della. "Oh, no thank you, my dear. I'm not very hungry."

Granny Little took a deep breath. "Do you know I have my eightieth birthday coming up?" she asked.

"Why, yes!" said Della. "Dinky and I think that's just wonderful!"

"Well, I don't," Granny Little said.

"Cousin Dinky is going to write a new

song in honor of your birthday!" said Lucy.

"Lucy!" said Mrs. Little. "That's supposed to be a secret."

"Oh my goodness," said Granny Little. "I never heard of anything more silly — writing a special song for an old lady."

"A very *special* lady," said Cousin Dinky.

"Fiddlesticks!" said Granny Little. "I never did anything special in my life!"

By this time most of the Littles were laughing to themselves. Cousin Dinky had a bad singing voice. He didn't know it because no one ever told him. Granny Little didn't know it because she was hard of hearing. And when Cousin Dinky's new wife, Della, saw how much he enjoyed singing, she never told him he had a bad voice either.

After the meal Mrs. Little kept Granny Little busy in the dining room. The others talked quietly in the living room about the suprise party.

"I think it's wonderful that the old folks in the valley agreed to fly to the party in my glider," said Cousin Dinky. "But I'm worried about using *The Nick of Time* to fly them in. There are some real problems."

"Why is that, Dinky?" asked Uncle Pete. "All of us thought it was a good idea."

"Well, it is a *glider* after all, Uncle Pete," said Cousin Dinky. "Once in a while the wind dies down to nothing and I have to land wherever I happen to be. It might be dangerous if I had to bring the glider down in the woods, for instance."

"Sometimes Dinky can't find a place to land when the wind dies," said Della. "Then he has to parachute from the glider."

"I see what you mean, Dinky," said Mr. Little. "There *are* problems."

"So — we're not going to have a party! I knew it!" Lucy stamped her foot.

"Gee," said Tom. "It's too bad we can't use Henry Bigg's gas model airplane. That would never come down if the wind went away."

"That's out of the question, Tom," said Mr. Little. "It's fairly new. It'll be a long time before Henry's ready to throw it away."

Cousin Dinky's eyes opened wide. He sat up straight. "I didn't know Henry had an airplane. Where does he keep it?"

"On his windowsill, mostly," Tom said.

"Aha, near the window," said Cousin Dinky.

"Hold on there, Dinky!" said Uncle Pete. "What are you getting at? If you're thinking what I'm thinking you're thinking — it would be too dangerous!"

"Dinky, do you mean to *take* Henry's plane?" said Mr. Little.

"I'm thinking we could *borrow* Henry's

plane for a good night's work," said Cousin Dinky. "We could easily fly all the old folks in one night and still get the airplane back on the windowsill before Henry woke up in the morning. The next night we could borrow it again and take them back."

Uncle Pete got up and began walking back and forth. "At least it's an *idea!*" he said. "And we are in trouble if we don't find a way to get the old folks to the party. But how in the world are we going to get the plane out of, and back into, Henry's room?"

"Don't worry about that, Uncle Pete," said Della. "Dinky will think of something!"

Cousin Dinky winked at his wife.

Just then Granny Little came into the room. She saw the look that passed between the newlyweds. "Sing us a song, Dinky," she said. "Do you know any love songs?"

Uncle Pete moved quickly toward the door. "Excuse me," he said. "I just remembered there was something terribly important I have to do."

Tom hopped up and ran after his uncle. "Me too, Uncle Pete! Wait for me!"

As they went out the door, Tom told Uncle Pete, "I *hate* love songs!"

"I figure we can come back in about ten minutes," said Uncle Pete. "Dinky doesn't usually sing for longer than that, thank heavens!"

THE next morning Tom and Lucy went to watch the Biggs eat breakfast. They were checking to see how much cereal was left in the box with the finger puppets on it.

But the Biggs weren't eating cereal. They were having eggs.

"Aw, do I have to eat eggs, Mom?" asked Henry Bigg. "I like cereal." He looked up at the box of cereal on the shelf.

"Henry," said Mrs. Bigg, "some people

would give anything to have eggs for breakfast *every* morning."

"I would give anything *not* to have eggs every morning," said Henry.

Mr. Bigg laughed. "We don't have eggs every morning, Henry."

"Seems like we do," said Henry. "I never knew six chickens could lay so many eggs."

"How many eggs in the hen-house this morning, Henry?" said Mr. Bigg.

"Four!" Henry said. "Worse than usual. Usually there are three."

"Henry, getting those chickens was one of the best ideas you ever had," said Mr. Bigg. "Why, these eggs are fresh laid — they're all good! Not like eggs you get at the store, some good and some bad." Mr. Bigg finished his egg. He smacked his lips. "Umm . . . delicious!"

"I thought having chickens would be fun!" Henry said. "It's no fun at all.

Chickens are dumb! All they ever do is lay eggs!"

Early the next morning, while it was still dark, Tom woke up Lucy. "It's time," he said.

Lucy dressed quickly and met her brother in the wall passageway outside the apartment.

"Hurry!" said Tom. "We've got to get back before the Biggs wake up." He ran to the tin-can elevator with Lucy behind him.

"Are you sure your idea will work, Tom?" asked Lucy as they rode the elevator to the basement of the Biggs' house.

"It's got to work," said Tom. "We want those finger puppets, don't we?"

Lucy nodded.

"Well, if the Biggs keep eating eggs, they'll never finish the cereal in time for us to get the puppets and rehearse for the play," Tom said.

The two children left the house by a secret door known only to the Littles. They crossed the driveway near the garage to the chicken yard. It was a part of the yard that Mr. Bigg had fenced off for the chickens and the hen-house.

It was easy for Tom and Lucy to slip through the chicken wire fence into the yard. "Sh!" said Tom. "We don't want to scare the chickens."

They entered the hen-house through a crack in the wall.

"It's dark!" said Lucy.

"Our eyes will get used to the dark in a while," said Tom. He pointed to a dusty window. "We'll get some moonlight."

They waited. Sure enough, after a few minutes the children began to make out shapes inside the shed. All the chickens were sitting on a roost at one end of the shed.

Tom pointed to another part of the

room. "That row of boxes are the nests," he said. "That's where they lay their eggs."

Hand in hand the children tiptoed toward the nests.

"Cluck, cluck!" said one of the hens.

Tom and Lucy stopped.

"Cluck, cluck!" another hen joined in.

The children hurried on. They got to the first nest and climbed in.

Most of the hens were clucking now.

Tom found an egg in the straw of the nest.

"What'll we do with it?" Lucy said.

"Hide it, of course," said Tom. "When Henry comes to get the eggs for breakfast, there won't be any. Then, they'll *have* to eat the cereal."

"Good!"

Tom looked around. "We need a hiding place nearby so we can get the eggs back in the nest after we get the cereal box."

Lucy pointed to a shelf behind the nests.

"That's good!" Tom said. If they could get the egg up there, they could roll it along the shelf. Then they could hide it behind one of those boards nailed to the wall.

All of the hens were scared now. "CLUCK, CLUCK!!" they went. Some of them flew down from the roost.

The children tried to pick up the egg. It was smooth and hard to handle. Tom couldn't quite get his arms around it.

By now the hens were squawking loudly and fluttering about the henhouse.

Tom knew that the Biggs would soon hear the noise the hens were making. When they did, Tom was sure they would come looking to see what was wrong. "Nuts!" he cried. "We don't have time!"

"Let's bury the egg in the straw, anyway," Lucy said. "Maybe they won't see it."

"Good idea!" said Tom. He began to dig a hole in the straw next to the egg.

"I'll get another one," said Lucy. She climbed into the next nest.

The hens were running around the hen-house, bumping into one another, and clucking.

Now Tom rolled the egg into the hole and covered it with straw. There was still time. He pulled himself up on the shelf behind the nests. He ran past Lucy. She was busy piling straw on the egg in that nest. Tom hurried toward the next nest.

Just then the hen-house door flew open. A blinding light filled the room.

Tom ran for cover behind a board.

Lucy had no time to get out of the nest. She dived into a corner and dug herself into the straw as far as she could. Then she pulled some straw over herself and lay still.

IT was Mr. Bigg and Henry.

Mr. Bigg shone his flashlight around the room. "Count the chickens, Henry!" he said.

"They're all here!" Henry said.

"Must be some kind of an egg-stealing animal got in here then," said Mr. Bigg.

The chickens kept right on clucking and fluttering about.

Henry ran from nest to nest. "Only one egg!" he said. "It must have got the others."

"I'll get some traps," said Mr. Bigg.

"We'll have to put them in places where the chickens can't get to."

Then Mr. Bigg pointed his flashlight straight into one of the nests. "Look at that!" he said. "There's something white under the straw in this one." He flicked away the straw with a stick. "Well! It's an egg!"

Henry laughed. "These hens are cuckoo!" he said. "They're burying their eggs." He ran from nest to nest sticking his hand into the straw. He found the other hidden egg.

"And you said your chickens were dumb, Henry," said Mr. Bigg.

"They are!" Henry said. "They're burying their eggs!"

"Maybe they were trying to hide their eggs from the egg stealer," Mr. Bigg said. "Did you think of that?"

"Gee — no," said Henry. "Boy! I guess I was wrong. These chickens of mine are really something!"

Later, when the Littles were having breakfast, Mr. Little said, "Henry's chickens made a big racket last night."

Tom shot a look at Lucy.

"They made so much noise," said Mr. Little, "that Mr. Bigg and Henry went to the hen-house to see what was going on."

Uncle Pete yawned. "I didn't hear a thing. When was that?"

"Before dawn," Mr. Little said. "I watched Mr. Bigg and Henry eat an early breakfast at about 5:30."

Tom shook his head. "I suppose they had eggs," he said. He made a face.

"Why, no, as a matter of fact," said Mr. Little. "They finished off a box of cereal between them. But, why do you ask, Tom?"

Mr. Little never got an answer to his question. Tom and Lucy were gone from the room almost before he asked it.

FOR the next few days the Littles worked hard to get ready for the surprise party.

It didn't rain, so they had to think of a way to fill the rain gutter for their new swimming pool. Luckily the Littles knew so much about the Biggs' house that a job like this was not a problem. They knew all about the water pipes — and the electric wiring too. The Littles kept the wires and pipes inside the walls in good repair, but the Biggs never knew it. The Littles were proud that they often did the repair work before the Biggs knew there was anything wrong.

One of the important plumbing jobs was to keep the pipes from rusting. The Littles worked hard at this. They were always polishing and scrubbing them.

The year before, Uncle Pete found a pipe with a bad rusty spot on it. It was on a cold-water pipe near the porch. Somehow the Littles had missed seeing it for a long time. For, when Uncle Pete scraped away the rust, it made a small hole in the pipe.

Before too much water leaked out, Uncle Pete stopped up the leak with chewing gum. Then he tied the hole tightly with some steel thread from a steel wool pad. He sealed it all up with wax from a birthday candle.

"Remember that leak I found last year?" said Uncle Pete. "We'll open that up again. Then we can pipe water from the leak to the rain gutter — and there's our swimming pool!"

"But how can we pipe it?" Mr. Little asked.

"We'll use Tom's idea," said Uncle Pete. "Plastic straws fitted together end to end."

Tom and Lucy were busy with the Little Red Riding Hood play. They found the empty cereal box in the trash can. The puppets on the box could be punched out along the dotted lines. It was hard work for the tiny children, but they got the job done.

By Sunday afternoon the children and Uncle Pete had practiced the play three times. Uncle Pete played the part of the

wolf. He growled and snapped and howled even when he wasn't supposed to.

Mrs. Little kept busy trying to find enough food for the picnic. They were expecting at least twenty-five people. Tom and Lucy said they wanted hot dogs. Mrs. Little was hoping that Mrs. Bigg was planning to have hot dogs for her Fourth-of-July picnic.

Mr. Little made an outdoor grill. He used two inches of window screening and the cap from a mustard jar. He managed to pick up some charcoal dust near Mr. Bigg's bag of charcoal.

Cousin Dinky set himself the job of finding a way to get Henry Bigg's airplane to the roof. He wanted to use the roof as a landing field just as he did for his glider flights.

The first thing Cousin Dinky and Della did was to borrow a ball of string from Mrs. Bigg. By using two empty thread-spools as pulleys, they made a block and tackle. A block and tackle would make it easier to lift the heavy airplane to the roof.

By Sunday evening Cousin Dinky and Della had tied the block and tackle to the TV antenna. Part of the antenna hung over the roof just above Henry's window. When they were ready to get the airplane, they would lower the string to the window.

All the Littles were ready for the great day. All except Granny Little, of course. She sat in her rocking chair, watching Baby Betsy in her playpen, wishing tomorrow would never come.

IT was midnight. Cousin Dinky, Uncle
Pete, Mr. Little, and Tom were on the
Biggs' roof. All of the Biggs were asleep.
A candle was fastened to the chimney
for light.

Cousin Dinky had made a loop on the
end of the string of the block and tackle.
He sat in the loop like sitting in a swing,
his feet just touching the roof.

"I'm ready," said Cousin Dinky. "Let's
start the operation. As soon as I get there,
I'll give one jerk on the string. Then,
when you feel two jerks, you can pull up
the plane."

"Good luck, Dinky," said Mr. Little.

Uncle Pete and Mr. Little got hold of the string. Cousin Dinky stepped off the roof. He swung out until he was under the antenna.

Tom whistled. "Wow! That looks like fun!"

Cousin Dinky gave the "thumbs up" signal. Mr. Little and Uncle Pete let the string go slowly through their hands. Cousin Dinky disappeared into the darkness below the roof.

"Dinky's block and tackle works well," said Uncle Pete. "You can hardly feel his weight."

"The plane will be heavier. Tom — you'll have to help us on that," said Mr. Little.

Tom looked over the edge of the roof. "Boy! It's black down there!" he said. "I can't see Cousin Dinky at all."

There was a tug on the string. Mr. Little and Uncle Pete stopped lowering it.

"He's at the window," whispered Uncle
Pete. "Good man!"

They waited. A bat flashed overhead. A
soft wind stirred the candle.

After a few minutes: two tugs on the
string.

"That didn't take long," Uncle Pete said.

The three Littles began pulling in the string. The work went fast.

"This airplane is lighter than anything," said Tom. "It must be made of aluminum."

In a few moments Cousin Dinky came up out of the darkness. He was sitting alone in the loop on the end of the string. There was no plane.

"What happened?" asked Mr. Little.

"Henry's airplane is not on the windowsill!" said Cousin Dinky. "It's high up on a shelf!"

"That Henry double-crossed us!" Tom cried.

"Oh my!" said Mr. Little. "I certainly didn't expect this. What will we do now?"

"We need that airplane!" Uncle Pete said.

"I know how we can get it, Uncle Pete," said Cousin Dinky. "But it will take perfect teamwork."

AN hour later the Littles were in Henry Bigg's bedroom.

Cousin Dinky, Uncle Pete, and Mr. Little were on the high shelf with Henry's gas model airplane. Tom was standing on Henry's pillow. Henry was asleep.

Lucky for the Littles, the Bigg boy kept a small night light on. It helped them to see in the darkened room.

There were two monster models on the shelf with Henry's airplane. One was King Kong, the ape monster. The other was Frankenstein's monster. Henry had made them from monster kits. The three Littles pushed and hauled the models to one end of the shelf.

Then they towed the airplane to that end of the shelf too. They turned the plane so that it was facing the empty shelf. It looked like a real airplane facing a runway, ready to take off.

Mr. Little and Uncle Pete put two dominoes in front of the wheels of the plane. They knelt beside them under the wing.

"All set, Dinky," whispered Mr. Little.

Cousin Dinky climbed into the cockpit of Henry's airplane. He checked the controls to be sure he knew how to start the engine. Then he leaned out of the cockpit, looked down at Tom on the bed, and whistled softly.

Tom took a ball of cotton from inside his shirt. He tiptoed close to Henry's ear. The plan was to stuff Henry's ears with cotton. Then he wouldn't hear the engine when Cousin Dinky flew the airplane out the window. It was a risky plan. The Littles thought it would work, because Henry was a heavy sleeper.

Henry was lying on his side. One of his ears was pressed into the pillow. "I only need to stuff one ear," thought Tom.

Slowly, slowly and gently, Tom lowered the cotton ball toward Henry's ear.

The cotton brushed lightly against the boy's ear. It tickled him. Still asleep, Henry moved his arm to scratch his tickly ear. Tom fell back on the pillow to keep from being struck by Henry's huge hand.

Tom tried a second time, slowly and gently.

This time the ticklish cotton woke Henry up. He scratched his ear, then sat up in bed. Tom leaped back away from Henry. He hid under the corner of the pillow.

In the meantime, Cousin Dinky had been watching what happened to Tom. He held his breath and prayed for Tom to get away safely.

Suddenly Henry got out of his bed and walked from the bedroom.

"Henry is going to the bathroom!" Cousin Dinky thought. "Now's our chance. I can fly out of here before he gets back!"

As soon as Cousin Dinky heard the bathroom door close, he started up the engine. In the quiet of Henry's room it sounded as loud as thunder to the Littles.

The airplane stood steady. It was held back by the dominoes against the wheels.

Cousin Dinky gave the "thumbs up" signal. Mr. Little and Uncle Pete pulled the dominoes out from in front of the wheels.

Henry's little airplane shot across the shelf and into the air. In a few seconds, Cousin Dinky circled the room once. Then he dived down and flew through the open bedroom window.

JULY the Fourth was a perfect day. It was sunny but not too hot. A light breeze cooled things off even more. Many of Granny Little's friends and relatives were on the roof of the Biggs' porch. They were waiting to surprise her.

Inside the walls of the house, Mrs. Little was putting the fifth diaper of the morning on Baby Betsy.

"There!" said Mrs. Little. She stood up from the match-box cradle. "Betsy — sometimes I think you're a fountain!"

Granny Little was sitting in her rocking chair, a dress for Baby Betsy in her lap. Every day for two weeks she got the dress out to work on it, then didn't. "Where's everybody?" asked Granny Little.

Mrs. Little took a deep breath. "They're all on the roof," she said. She tried hard not to show Granny Little how excited she was.

"Whatever for?" Granny Little asked.

"Because it's a perfectly beautiful day," said Mrs. Little. She bent over and picked up Baby Betsy. "I'm going up myself. Won't you come too?"

"Oh my, no," said Granny Little. "That's no place for an eighty-year-old. Maybe eight or eighteen or twenty-eight — but not eighty!"

"Granny — I'm surprised at you," said Mrs. Little. "You are usually so adventurous, so willing to try something new. This isn't like you at all."

"I'm coming to my senses!" said

Granny Little. "A person eighty years old is old! They've no business gallivanting around like young folks. They should stay home. Nobody wants to see them anyway."

"Your family are all on the porch roof sitting in the shade of the catalpa tree. There are beautiful blossoms all over the tree — "

Granny Little interrupted. "*I* remember when that tree first came up. Do you mean to tell me that it's already shading the roof?"

Mrs. Little reached for Granny Little's hand. "Come and see it. The children want to have a picnic. They'd love it if you would come up."

"Picnics are for young people," said Granny Little. She picked up the dress for Baby Betsy. "I'll stay here and work on this dress if you don't mind."

Mrs. Little carried her baby across the room. "Oh well, maybe you'll come up a little later." She shook her head and left the room.

In a few minutes Cousin Dinky came into the living room. "How about taking a ride in my glider, Granny?" he asked.

Granny Little put her hand behind her ear to hear better. She laughed. "My ears are bothering me, Dinky," she said. "I thought I heard you ask me to take a ride in your glider."

"I did!" said Cousin Dinky. "It's a beautiful day. The wind is perfect. I'll show you the Biggs' house from the air."

Granny Little put Baby Betsy's dress on the table next to her chair. She stood up. "I've always wanted to take a ride in that glider of yours, Dinky. You know that. Wait — I'll get my hat."

Cousin Dinky put his arm around the old lady. "You won't need a hat," he said. "I have a flier's helmet with goggles for you to wear." He walked with Granny Little to the door.

Granny Little stopped suddenly. She turned and looked at Cousin Dinky. "I'm eighty years old today," she said. "Do you think that's too old to fly in a glider?"

"You know me," said Cousin Dinky. "Why in the world would I think such a thing as that?"

"Oh, I don't know," said Granny Little. "You have to stop doing new things sometime in your life, don't you?"

"I'm not going to," said Cousin Dinky. "If I live to be one hundred years old, I'm still going to have adventures."

Granny Little laughed. "One hundred!" she said. "Why, *that's* old! I've got a long time to go before I reach that!"

"Come with me, Granny," said Cousin Dinky. "Before we go up in the glider, there's something I want you to see on the roof."

"SURPRISE!!"

"Happy Birthday!!"

"Hooray for Granny Little!!"

"Oh my!" said Granny Little. "Oh my, oh my!"

Granny Little stood under the catalpa tree on the Biggs' roof. Surrounding her were twenty-four friends and relatives. The old woman looked from face to face. They were all smiling at her.

For a moment Granny Little couldn't say a word. At last she spoke: "Oh my goodness," she said. "What a surprise. You shouldn't surprise an old woman so."

Lucy Little stood by Granny Little's side looking up at her. "You really were surprised, weren't you, Granny?" she said.

"Oh dear me," said Granny Little. "All these dear people are here for my birthday. I just can't believe it. I must be dreaming."

"It's true!" Mrs. Little said. "They're all here to wish you a very special eightieth birthday."

"Well, this will only happen once in my life," said Granny Little. "I'd better enjoy it."

One by one the old woman greeted her friends and relatives. "Here's Cousin Emma. How are you, dear?" said Granny Little. "It's been so many years since we've seen each other." She hugged the woman.

Granny Little moved to the next person. "And — oh how wonderful! It's Brenda — the maid of honor at my wedding! What a surprise to see you, Brenda!"

Then came Granny Little's older sister: "Littebit!! How brave of you to come all this way!" She turned to Mrs. Little. "My sister lives *three* blocks away!"

"I know," said Mrs. Little, who was delighted.

And so on from cousin to nieces to nephews to childhood friends and finally, "But where's Zelda?" Granny Little stood on her toes and looked around. "Where's my old friend, Zelda Short?"

"She wouldn't come, Granny," said Mrs. Little.

"At the last minute she was too scared to fly with me in Henry's airplane," said Cousin Dinky.

"Fly? She could walk, couldn't she?" asked Granny Little.

"Zelda says she's too old to gallivant around all over the place," said Uncle Pete. He winked at Mr. Little.

"Too old!" said Granny Little. There was excitement in her eyes. "Why that's nonsense! Look at all these wonderful people. They're not too old! And some of them are older than I am too. They came! Zelda should be here. We're going to have a ball!"

"That's telling her, Granny!" said Uncle Pete.

Granny Little looked around at all the smiling faces. Suddenly she said, "Dinky — get that helmet and goggles you promised me! We're going to fly to the Shorts and bring Zelda back with us."

"But, Granny," said Dinky, grinning, "she won't come."

"She'll come all right," Granny Little said. "We just won't let her sit there and say 'no'!"

"THANK you, Mr. Little," said Zelda
Short. "I would like just a bit more of that
delicious hot dog, if you please." She
smiled at Granny Little who sat nearby.
"I'm so glad you made me come, dear,"
she said. "This is the best party. I'm having the time of my life."

"I knew," said Granny Little, "that if
you could just keep your eyes closed all
the time you were up in the air, you
would make the trip all right."

It was the middle of the afternoon. The surprise party was in full swing. Just as Mrs. Little hoped, the Biggs were having hot dogs. The Littles managed to find a slightly burned hot dog the Biggs didn't use. Even with part of the hot dog burned, there was plenty left for the tiny people.

The guests sat on the porch roof under the catalpa tree. There were red and white tablecloths for some people and blue and white tablecloths for others. The Littles had made them from some old bandanas that Henry Bigg no longer wore.

"It's a real red, white, and blue Fourth of July!" Uncle Pete said. "Hooray for the American Revolution!"

"Were there tiny people back in those days, Uncle Pete?" asked Lucy.

"There sure were, Lucy," said Uncle Pete. "Some of them worked nights to help Betsy Ross finish the first American flag. George Washington wanted it in a hurry, you remember. Of course, no one knew the tiny people helped. Betsy Ross herself could never figure out how she got it made so fast."

The birthday cupcake was cut and everyone had a piece. Then Granny Little opened her presents.

She especially liked the feather pillow that Lucy made from Henry Bigg's blue jay feather.

"It's beautifully sewed, Lucy," said Granny Little.

Lucy was proud. She beamed at her mother.

Tom's present was a chocolate kiss wrapped in silver foil.

"I'll never be able to eat all this, Tom," said Granny Little.

"Tom will help you!" said Uncle Pete and everybody laughed.

Mr. and Mrs. Little gave the old woman a sterling silver thimble waste-basket.

"Mr. Little found it in the back yard when the Biggs were digging up the sewer pipes," said Mrs. Little. "We think it may be very old."

Uncle Pete gave Granny Little a coin purse to use as a knitting bag. "I know it's a little large," he said.

"It's perfect, Peter," said Granny Little, kissing him.

There were many other gifts from Granny Little's friends and relatives. One of her favorites was the eighty violets the Small family picked on the way to the party.

After that everyone sat down to watch the Little Red Riding Hood play.

Uncle Pete, who had done so well during practice, forgot many of his lines. Whenever he couldn't remember them he growled and howled like a wolf, hoping no one would notice.

Tom and Lucy whispered the lines to Uncle Pete. Everyone could hear the whispering except Granny Little. They were laughing. "I don't know what you were all laughing about," said Granny Little when the play was over. "It was a very dramatic show, and not a bit funny." She patted Uncle Pete's shoulder. "Peter Little, you're quite an actor. I heard every line you said as clear as a bell."

After the play many people went swimming in the rain gutter swimming pool. Uncle Pete rigged up a tongue depressor to use as a diving board.

Once, during the afternoon, Uncle Pete did a belly-whopper into the pool. Some

of the water splashed down into the Biggs' yard as Mr. Bigg was walking by. It fell on his bare head.

"Golly," said Mr. Bigg. "It's starting to rain." He called his family to come in out of the rain.

Finally it was time for Cousin Dinky to pick up his guitar and sing the song he had written for Granny Little.

Most of the guests had heard Cousin Dinky sing in their own homes. They knew the awful truth about his singing. But they were very brave. Not one person sneaked away. Everyone stayed and listened to the song, probably out of respect for Granny Little.

This is what they heard Cousin Dinky
sing:

Although you sometimes think you're old,
Don't let your age mislead you.
You, it's true, depend on us,
But, Granny, how we need you!

Your ready smile, your helping hands
Have shown us all the right way
To live our lives in four score years
To make each day a bright day.

You've knit for us and darned our socks
And told us old-time stories.
Now we celebrate your day —
the Fourth and all its glories!

So, happy birthday, dear Granny!
Happy birthday to you.

"What a wonderful song!" said Granny
Little. "And what a wonderful surprise
party. I'll never forget it as long as I live!"